PEANUT

Linas Alsenas

SCHOLASTIC PRESS 🥜 NEW YORK

Mildred was lonely.

One day she found a stray...

...puppy.

She decided to bring him home.

Mildred tried to feed the puppy dog food,

and she offered him a bone, but the puppy seemed to like only one thing.

So Mildred named him Peanut.

Peanut was quite useful around the apartment. He watered Mildred's plants.

He was a great couchwarmer.

And he was terrific at squashing cereal boxes.

On sunny days, Mildred took Peanut for walks in the park.

He was different from the other dogs.

Peanut didn't roll over.

He never fetched.

And he didn't bark...exactly.

Even so, Mildred loved Peanut dearly.

One day, a man from the circus stopped Mildred in the park. "Madam," he cried, "you have found our missing elephant!"

He thanked her and
took Peanut away.

Mildred missed Peanut very much.
She decided to go to the circus.

Peanut was very happy
to see her...

...but Mildred could see
that he liked being home.

After the circus left town,
Mildred was lonely once again.

Then one day, she found a stray...

...kitten.

She decided to
bring him home.

To my father, Paul Alsenas, for seeing horses in cow pastures

L. A.

Library of Congress Data is available
ISBN-13: 978-0-439-77980-7 · ISBN-10: 0-439-77980-4
Printed in Singapore 46 · First edition, August 2007

The display type is set in Circus Mouse. The text type is set in Chowderhead. Book design by Richard Amari